make friends
BREAK friends

Other books by Julia Jarman:

make Friends
BREAK Friends

Julia Jarman

Illustrated by
Kate Pankhurst

Andersen Press · London

First published in 2013 by
Andersen Press Limited
20 Vauxhall Bridge Road
London SW1V 2SA
www.andersenpress.co.uk

4 6 8 10 9 7 5 3

British Library Cataloguing in Publication Data available.

ISBN 978 1 84939 509 0

Printed and bound in Great Britain
by CPI Group (UK) Ltd, Croydon, CR0 4YY

To Daisy who helped a lot.

Daisy

Daisy is friendly and gets on with
everyone. She's kind and sensible. She's
always thinking of how she can help others
and loves being a school 'buddy'. She hates
it when people fall out and was very upset
when her parents split up, though
she's got used to it now.

Phoebe

Phoebe is shy and finds it hard to
make friends. She enjoys craft which
she can do on her own – but it's even
better with Daisy. And Daisy shares her love
of reading. She likes the peace and quiet
of Daisy's house, where they can get on
without being disturbed by Phoebe's
little brothers, The Smellies.

Erika

Erika is entertaining. She's full
of energy and very sporty. She means
well but sometimes doesn't realise she's
hurting people's feelings. She tries very
hard to please her parents who expect
her to be good at everything, and
sometimes that's a strain.

Daisy

'What's wrong, Phoebe?' I asked. But I knew what it was.

This was about Erika and what happened after school today.

Please don't cry. Phoebe looked like a hurt puppy, hair flopping over her sad brown eyes.

'Well, let's do something,' I said briskly. 'It'll be ages before tea's ready.'

Mum was crashing around in the kitchen, still doing the breakfast pots most likely.

'What do you want to do?'

'I don't mind.'

Phoebe *never* minds. It's irritating.

'Let's do our collage then.'

Our under-the-sea scene was coming along really well and Phoebe smiled.

'That's what you wanted to do all along, isn't it?'

She nodded.

'So why didn't you *say?*'

Laughing, she delved into her bag and brought out some great bits of shiny material and some gauzy see-through stuff, and soon we were cutting and sticking away. I found some bits of burst balloon.

'Octopus!' we yelled at the same time.

Sometimes it's like that with Phoebe and me. We're completely on the same wavelength and don't even need to talk. We're definitely best friends. Well, I'm her only friend, actually, and that's the trouble. I'm friends with everyone, but she HATES me playing or even talking to anyone else. It drives me crazy.

'Phoebe, I was talking to Erika after school because she was upset.'

Erika had missed an open goal and the netball team had lost.

'It's my job to help people. You know that.'

I'm a school 'buddy', which means I have to help kids who are upset.

'It's your job to help people who are being *bullied*, Daisy. Erika wasn't being bullied.'

True. No one would bully Erika. She's popular and ever so funny. It's the faces she pulls. Even teachers can't help laughing. Everyone likes Erika.

Except Phoebe.

'Erika wasn't keen on going home,' I said. 'You know what her mum's like at matches.'

She SHOUTS. Today's match was in the dinner hour so she hadn't come, but Erika was dreading telling her the result.

Phoebe carried on sticking.

'So that's why I stayed talking to *her* instead of walking straight home with you.'

Phoebe and I live just round the corner from one another, but before Mum and Dad split up I lived nearer Erika. We were best friends then. Still are, in a way, but it's not the same.

She used to come round mine a lot.

'It doesn't mean I don't like *you* if I talk to *her*. You're both my best friends.'

Phoebe kept quiet.

'Please.' I persisted. 'Don't go all droopy when I talk to Erika. You should try and see her good points.'

'Suppose so, but what about *her*? She gets stroppy if you talk to me.'

Actually, Phoebe had a point. Erika was just as bad. Worse in a way. Phoebe wilts like a flower out of water when I play with Erika. But if Erika sees me with Phoebe she explodes. *'What do you see in her?'* Sometimes those two make me feel like a ragdoll being torn apart by two little girls in the nursery.

Idea!

It came to me in a flash. *Why don't I stop them?* I mean, if I can get little kids who've been fighting to shake hands and make up, surely I can get my two best friends to like each other?

Suddenly I was determined. It was exactly what a buddy was for – to get everyone to be friendly. Phoebe was wrong. It wasn't just about stopping bullying. Right, I was on a mission now so I needed a plan . . .

One – talk to Phoebe about Erika. Well, I'd done that.

Two – talk to Erika about Phoebe. I'll do that as soon as I can.

Three – get them to talk to each other.

It couldn't be that hard, could it?

Phoebe

I really *really* don't want to fall out with Daisy, but *see Erika's good points?*

One – she's good at games – so?

Two – she's funny – if making fun of other people is funny.

She thinks she's hilarious if she's imitating the way someone walks or talks, but it's not *kind*. And she's got a temper. She explodes if someone just spells her name wrong. *'I'm Erika with a K!'*

Three – blank.

But I'll try and think of something because I love going round Daisy's house. It's great with just her and her mum. So quiet. Not like at mine with The Smellies bawling their heads off or charging around like little tanks.

They've just learned to crawl so it's worse now as they get into my things. Why did my mum have to go and have twins?

Daisy is the best friend I've ever had. She's kind and we enjoy the same things, like art and craft, and reading and Drama Club on Friday nights. I just hope Daisy doesn't want Erika to join in with what we do. Erika doesn't *join in*. She TAKES OVER. If Daisy tells Erika about Drama Club . . . well, I don't know what I'll do, but it'll ruin everything. I hate annoying Daisy by being 'droopy', as she calls it but I can't help it. When she goes off with Erika it *hurts*, I mean *really*. It's as if my insides get tied in tight little knots.

But I'll try – well, not to let it show – or Daisy might go off me. As long as she doesn't tell me and Erika to make up, like infants in the playground.

'Shake hands and make friends, girls.'

Daisy can be very – what's the word? – bossy.

And how can you have two best friends?

Erika

Daisy wants me to talk to Pheeble! She cornered me in the playground straight after dinners.

I said, 'What about, Dais? We've got nothing in common.'

'You've both got two little brothers.'

I mean, what's that got to do with anything? Mum says it's having brothers that's taught me to hold my own. But Pheeble can't hold anything, definitely not a ball. She's hopeless.

'I just want you two to get to know each other,' Daisy persisted.

'But *why?*' I'd told the boys I'd play football with them.

'Because . . .'

I put my arm round her shoulders. 'Because you're a busybody-buddy who wants everyone

12

to be luvvy-duvvy friends!'

Honestly, Daisy is so, well, *fluffy,* when she isn't being teacherish. I wish she still lived near me. It was great going round hers.

I said, 'OK, Dais, I'll promise to try and be nice to Pheeble.'

'*Don't* call her that!'

Oh, no! Now I'd upset her!

'She isn't feeble, Erika. You should get to know her and you'd see. Please, come and talk to her.'

Pheeble – whoops, Phoebe – was standing all alone by the fence.

'Not now, Dais, I promised the boys I'd play footie.'

'This afternoon then?' she persisted. 'Right?'

'Right.' I pulled my Daffy Duck face to cheer her up. 'Honest. I'll see you by the tree at playtime.'

Off at last. I must have crossed the playground in ten seconds flat.

13

I'll do my best but honestly I just can't see me and Phee— Whoops! – Phoebe having anything to say to each other.

Daisy

Well, I've made a start!

The meeting this afternoon went really well, thanks mostly to Erika, I have to say, though she was a bit late. I could feel Phoebe not wanting to be there, and thought she might even leave, but then Erika breezed in as friendly as anything. I was really proud of her.

'Hi, you guys! What's on the agenda?'

I had to laugh. 'It's not a council meeting, Erika!' We're both on the school council. 'But if you want to call it something I suppose it's friendship.'

I managed to explain that I like both of them and really like doing things with both of them, but it upsets me when they get jealous.

'Jealous?!' Erika wrinkled her nose. 'I'm not jealous of h—'

Phoebe went red.

'Well,' I said quickly, 'it doesn't matter what you call it. I just think it would help if you two got to know each other better.'

'OK.' Erika nodded. 'How?' She sounded really positive.

'Well, we could do things together.'

Phoebe nudged me then, but when I said, 'What is it, Phoebe?' she just looked at the ground.

Erika said, 'OK. What do you two like that I might like?'

Pause – because I suddenly realised why Phoebe nudged me. Did I really want Erika joining in with collage or jewellery-making or our reading club? Now *I* felt myself going red.

Fortunately Phoebe helped by saying, 'What do you like doing, Erika, besides sport I mean?'

And Erika said, 'Oh, lots of things.'

But then silence again.

It was all beginning to go negative, but luckily I had a brainwave. 'Tell you what, why don't we do things together in the playground? You've seen the new grids that they painted? Well, there are all these new games we can play.'

Actually they're mostly old games, like our grannies played when they were young, but they're good fun. All the buddies have learned the rules so we can teach everyone else.

Well, we ended up playing hopscotch and Erika was best, of course, but Phoebe tried and we had some laughs.

So, fingers crossed.

Phoebe

I don't like saying this but sometimes Daisy just doesn't get it. She thinks everyone is as nice as they *seem*, and Erika isn't. Daisy thought the 'meeting' yesterday went really well. When Erika raced off she said, 'See, she was really nice!'

Well, yes, she was sort of. But by afternoon break today she was back to her old self.

Erika led her fan club into the playground. Daisy and I followed, and suddenly Erika's shouting, 'Let's play tag!' and doing 'Out scout, you're out' very fast.

Next thing I'm 'It' – surprise surprise – and she's yelling, 'Count to ten, Phoebe!' and everyone else is running away.

So there I am standing in the middle of the playground feeling, well, got at. I just knew Erika had made me 'It' on purpose, and I think

Daisy thought so too because she suddenly ran towards me.

'Tag me,' Daisy whispered. And I was going to, but then someone – no guesses who – grabs her arm and pulls her away.

'Run, Phoebe! You're supposed to run after people!' No guesses who that was, either.

But I couldn't. I just couldn't.

I know that does sound feeble but I was ever so tired. The Smellies had been bawling their heads off half the night, and I knew there was no point. I'm hopeless at running at the best of times – and, well, I didn't mean to, but I started crying in front of *everyone*, and I could feel them all staring at me.

Then Erika shouted, 'Don't be feeble, Pheeble!'

And everyone started laughing.

They *screeched* with laugher.

Everyone. Even Daisy. I saw her.

The laughing went on for ages and ages till Mrs Davies came out and sent them all inside.

Daisy

I can't believe what's just happened.

I can't believe Erika shouted what she did.

I can't believe Phoebe didn't try *at all*. She *was* feeble. I tried to help her by getting near her but she just stood there with her arms stuck out like, like a daft *windmill*.

Erika was horrible, I have to admit, but ever so funny – she pulled a face just like Phoebe's and stuck out her arms just like her – and, well, I couldn't help laughing. I *wasn't* laughing at Phoebe, I was laughing at Erika, but Mrs Davies thinks I was.

'I'm surprised at *you*, Daisy.' That's what she said before she yelled at everyone to go and stand outside her room. Then she went over to Phoebe.

Well, I just wanted to melt away. I felt sick.

Honestly, I'd have done anything to rewind the last few minutes and do it differently. But all I could do was walk up to Phoebe and say sorry. She just sobbed, 'Go away, Daisy. I thought you were my friend.'

For once Phoebe *did* mind.

And so did Mrs Davies. She shook her head and said, 'We'll talk about this later, Daisy. Go and stand with the others for the time being.'

I know she thinks I'm as bad as the others.

I'm sure she'll say I can't be a buddy any more.

Buddies are supposed to be kind!

Erika

Eeek!

I'm not sure what happened there, but I really, really didn't mean it to go like that. I chose Phoebe as 'It' to get her to join in. Honest. I was only trying to do what Daisy asked.

I just hope I managed to convince Mrs Davies, but it didn't help that Daisy looked as if she'd trodden on a kitten. I explained that it had been Daisy's idea to get Phoebe to join in more, and that I was trying to help.

Mrs D said, 'But what about the name-calling?'

'That just slipped out, Mrs Davies. A joke.'

'A cruel joke, Erika.'

I said, 'Sorry, Mrs Davies. I'll say sorry to Phoebe too.'

'Good. I'm sure you meant well, Erika.'

Exactly.

Actually I think Mrs D knows Phoebe needs to toughen up a bit. Just wish I could convince Daisy-Down-in-the-Dumps.

I tried to cheer her up when we got back to class.

'We've all apologised, Dais.' I'd organised that straight after register. 'What more can we do?'

But she exploded: 'Get lost, Miss Popular!' and stropped off to help Pheeble with her science project. Next thing she's shouting at Pheeble.

And I saw why. Honestly, there's no helping some people.

Pheeble got five merit points for work *Daisy* had done and she wouldn't tell the teacher Daisy had helped her.

Daisy was really upset so I sent her a note, saying *Still rather be friends with HER?*. And she *tore it up*.

26

Honestly, I felt myself going red. Everyone was looking at me and one of the other girls said, 'You're not going to let her get away with that, are you?'

And I said, 'No, I'm not.'

I'm really not!

Phoebe

I still feel awful.

Things are even worse now.

Daisy says she wasn't laughing at me in the playground, but I saw her. And why did she say sorry if she didn't do anything?

I thought she wanted to make up because in the next lesson she was really nice – at first. When she'd finished her science folder she came to help me with mine. I didn't actually *need* help because I'd nearly finished, but I let her help so as not to hurt her feelings.

But then she hurt mine.

When Miss Perkins gave me five merit points and said she'd show my folder to Mrs Davies, Daisy was horrible.

'Tell her! Tell her I helped you!' She *screamed*.

Well, Miss Perkins had left the room so I couldn't go running after her. I don't even know why Daisy wanted me to. I suppose she's desperate to get in Mrs Davies's good books now that she's been told off for being mean. AND, another thing, I think Daisy is jealous. I didn't think she was like that.

Afterwards I saw Erika passing her a note, so it looks as if those two are best friends again now.

Erika *is* taking over, like I knew she would.

Daisy

This afternoon was terrible.

It was horrible being told off by Mrs Davies with all the other girls. Erika may have convinced Mrs Davies she 'meant well' by choosing Phoebe to be 'It', but I'm not so sure. She definitely wasn't when she called her Pheeble.

Anyway, after break, I just got on with my work, which was finishing off our science folders. At least you can get on with your work when no one's friends with you. Well, I took my folder to Miss Perkins who said it was the *best bit of science I'd ever done*. She said it was so good she'd show my folder to Mrs Davies and I'd probably get an achievement certificate for it. Me! An achievement certificate! Erika's always getting them for sporty stuff. Phoebe gets them for all her school work, but I've never *ever* had a single one.

Well, I was cheering up a bit and went to help Phoebe with her project. But things went wrong *again*. At the end of the lesson Miss Perkins gave Phoebe five merit points, picked up *her* folder to take to Mrs Davies and left mine on the desk. I said, 'Phoebe, go and tell Miss Perkins I helped you.' But she didn't. She wouldn't. She just stood there like a frightened rabbit.

I'm SO fed up with Phoebe doing nothing. It was the playground all over again, and Erika was watching. I could almost hear her saying *'Told you so, told you so'*. Next thing she's passing me a note: *Still rather be friends with HER?*.

Well, I was furious – with both of them – so I tore it up and she went off in a massive strop.

After dinners I sensed something was wrong as soon as I stepped into the playground. I looked around to see who was in trouble –

and there was Erika and her fan club staring at *me*.

I was in trouble, I could feel it. You know the expression 'looking daggers'? Well, I could feel the daggers sticking into me.

Then Erika said, 'We don't like Daisy today, do we?' And they all turned their backs on me.

All of them. I can't describe the feeling exactly but it was even worse than the dagger-looks. I wanted to get away but I couldn't move.

So I just stood there feeling dreadful – like Phoebe, I suppose – when one of the dinner ladies came up and said, 'Hello, Daisy, looking for your little friend? She's in the sick room. You can go and see her if you like.'

Did I want to see Phoebe? I did actually. I'd started to feel a bit bad for having a go at her. I mean, it wasn't her fault that Miss Perkins left my folder behind. *I* could have reminded her. So I headed for the sickroom to

say, 'Sorry, Phoebe', and, 'It doesn't matter', and, 'Let's be friends'. But when I got there it was too late. She'd gone. The secretary said her mum had picked her up.

'We don't like Daisy' went on all afternoon. None of the girls spoke to me, but Miss Perkins didn't seem to notice they were being mean. Luckily, at playtime I was on buddy duty in the infants' playground. I kept busy organising a game of French cricket for some of the boys, but I couldn't stop worrying.

'I'm surprised at *you*, Daisy.' Mrs Davies's words keep going over and over in my head.

I'm really worried she's going to stop me being a buddy.

Erika

I can't stop thinking about Daisy.

Maybe I was a bit mean at school today.

I'm sure she was crying when we all turned our backs on her.

Thing is, Daisy can't bear not being friends, and actually I don't like it, either. Maybe I did overreact, but it hurt when she tore up my note. In front of everyone! When I was trying to be friendly! I thought I might blub for a minute. Anyway, tomorrow I'll tell her I forgive her and call off 'Don't speak to Daisy', and tell her I'd like to do something with her and Phoebe – just like she said she wanted to.

That should sort it. I can see her face now, all pleased and grateful.

In fact there *is* something I'd like to do with her and Phoebe. Someone said they go to a

35

drama club on Friday nights. It's in a spooky old mill which has been converted into a theatre. Sounds really cool.

I'm going to write her a note NOW.

Thursday

Daisy

I can't *believe* Erika.

She's just given me a note saying *she's* forgiven *me* for tearing up her note! Well, you can guess what I did with that, so 'Don't talk to Daisy' is on again.

But I don't care. Well, not too much. If she thinks I'll ever be friends with her again, she's wrong, wrong, *wrong*. I'll never forgive her. Never! Phoebe's right. Erika *is* mean.

Trouble is I can't tell Phoebe because she's not here. She must still be sick. When I went round last night her mum said she'd gone to bed early. Or she's avoiding me. Phoebe's tummy aches are very convenient sometimes. Anyway, she wasn't waiting outside this morning and when I knocked on the door no one answered. Most likely no one heard. It sounded like a zoo inside. Her dad's car had gone, so at first I thought she'd had a lift to school but she wasn't in the playground when I got here.

I hope she isn't very ill.

Morning break wasn't as bad as it could have been. I went and sat on the buddy bench and Barney, who's in top class, joined me.

Barney goes to Drama Club too. It's at the Old Mill Theatre outside the village. It's not a school club. Barney was Joseph in *Joseph and his Amazing Technicolor Dreamcoat*. He's really nice and he told me something very interesting.

'Lenny says we're going to do another production, but don't tell anyone because he hasn't announced it yet.'

Lenny runs the club and Barney overheard him talking about it.

'What's the show going to be?'

'*The Wizard of Oz.*'

'Wow! Phoebe and I are reading that!'

'Cool,' he said. 'You'll know the characters really well and be great at auditions. Where is Phoebe, by the way?'

I didn't answer because I suddenly had a horrible thought. If Phoebe really has fallen

out with me I won't be able to get to Drama Club. If her mum won't take me in the car I won't be able to go.

I said, 'Can I tell Phoebe? She won't tell anyone.'

Barney laughed. 'She'd be perfect as Cowardly Lion, wouldn't she? And you'd make a great—'

But he didn't finish because Erika was rushing over.

'Hi, Daisy!' She slung her arm round me as if we were best friends. 'Hi, Barney! Tell us about this Drama Club. Can anyone join?'

Two-faced isn't the word!

I just hope Phoebe doesn't think I told her about it.

Friday

Phoebe

Daisy and I are friends again!

She came round last night and we made up. And we're going to Drama Club tonight – well, if Mum will take us. Trouble is Mum says I shouldn't go out tonight as I've been off school for two days with a bug. But I'm all right now and I've *got* to go or Daisy can't get there.

Daisy was bursting to tell me there's going to be a show. Actually, I'm not all that keen. The thing I like about Drama Club – it was such a relief when we first went – is that we *don't* have to perform. We don't even have to go on stage. We just get in pairs or groups and do improvisations, which means imagining ourselves in different situations.

I'm good at it, but if I had to do it on stage I'd die. I really would.

Still, I suppose I can say I'd rather work backstage. Yes, that's what I'll do. I'll volunteer to make props or help with the costumes. I could even design some. I'd like that.

I'm really enjoying *The Wizard of Oz*, reading the book I mean, and I've nearly finished it. Daisy thinks it's a bit slow, but I think it will make a great show, and she'd be ace as Dorothy. I'd just love her to get the main part so I'm going to try my hardest to persuade Mum to take us. In fact I'll remind Mum she owes Daisy. Mum had nagged me to join the Drama Club for ages – to *'bring me out'*, she said – but I didn't dare till Daisy said she'd go with me.

I'm so glad we're friends again.

Daisy

Trouble! Erika came to Drama Club last night!

I hadn't dared tell Phoebe that Erika had asked Barney about joining. I just hoped Erika would forget all about it, but when we got to the Old Mill she was there with a crowd around her, laughing at one of her jokes.

It was just like school.

'Hi, Daisy! Hi, Phoebe!' She waved when she saw us.

Well, Phoebe just froze in the doorway. I nearly had to drag her inside.

Still, I don't think Erika liked it much. I'm sure she was expecting to be a star, instantly. When Lenny asked us to get in twos and think of something we were scared of she started sucking her thumb and stuttering, 'I'm s-s-scared of the b-b-bogeyman.'

Everyone laughed till Lenny told us to go away and find a space and have a quiet think. Later, I saw Lenny having a word with her and guessed what he was saying. *'Stop playing to the gallery, Erika.'* That's what he says to anyone who's showing off and looking for applause.

Phoebe saw too but it didn't stop her wailing, *'Why* did you tell her?'

I said, 'I didn't – and, look, she probably won't come again now she's seen what it's like.'

If Lenny had told me off the first time I went I'd never have shown my face again.

But Erika's not like me – or anyone else I know. I suppose she's used to being criticised by her mother. Anyway, she was soon bouncing around again like Tigger!

Actually, and I couldn't say this to Phoebe, but a bit of me can't help admiring that.

Erika

Drama Club's great!

Well, it will be when we start rehearsing for a proper show. At first it was a bit boring because we did 'exploring your emotions' and everyone was dead serious, but then, halfway through, Lenny the director said we were going to do *The Wizard of Oz*, actually put it on for an audience! Well, I just LOVE that show and when I told Mum on the way home she said, 'You'd make a great Dorothy, darling.'

'But that's the main part, Mum, and I've only just started.'

'Aim high, darling. You don't want to be an also-ran, do you?'

Well, she's right, actually. I think I'm in with a chance because we've got the DVD and I've seen it hundreds of times. Also, well, I don't want to be big-headed, but none of the others seemed very good at acting. Except Barney, but he can't very well be Dorothy, can he?

Everyone was friendly except Daisy and Pheeb— Whoops! – Phoebe. They didn't seem at all pleased to see me, which was a bit off. I mean it was Daisy's idea that we started doing things together. Those two hold grudges. That's their trouble. Forgive and forget, that's what I say.

Anyway, the auditions are next week so I'm going to start practising.

Saturday

Phoebe

I'm up and down like a seesaw.

UP. I *do* want a part. I'll show Erika. She's *not* going to ruin Drama Club.

DOWN. I don't want to go any more.

Last night was just like school. Honestly, when I walked in and saw her there, the centre of attention already, I wanted to be sick. If it wasn't for Daisy I'd have stayed outside, but she said, 'Come *on* – unless you're determined to let her take over.'

But all night long I could feel her thinking I was rubbish.

But – UP – I *am* good at acting. I *can* imagine what it's like being someone else and that's what acting is, unless – DOWN – other people are watching.

But – UP– at least I'm not afraid of my own mother like someone I could mention.

Anyway, Lenny says we've all got to audition for a part, even if we do just want to work behind the scenes, so I'm going to have to try. And I'm going to help Daisy practise so she gets a good part. I'm going round hers this morning to discuss the characters. Daisy and I are going to act some bits out too.

Six days to find my courage!

Friday

A Week Later

Daisy

Auditions tonight!

I'm nervous but also quite optimistic because the rest of today was great. My confidence is well boosted. It started just after register when Miss Perkins said I'd got an achievement certificate for my science project! Really! She remembered, after all, with a bit of help from Phoebe she said. But Phoebe hadn't told me she'd reminded her.

'Phoebe, why didn't you tell me you'd told her?'

'So you'd get a surprise,' she said with this big smile on her face – till Erika came along to say congratulations.

I was scared of going to Mrs Davies's room to get it, but Phoebe came with me to get hers too, and Mrs Davies was really nice. I still thought she might say I couldn't be a buddy any more because I'd laughed at Phoebe, but she didn't.

She just said, 'It's good to see that you two are friends again.'

I said, 'We didn't stop being friends, Mrs Davies.'

I just wish I could say the same about Erika and Phoebe. My mission to get us all to be friends has failed miserably. It's the same old problem – I can be friends with one or the other. I mean Phoebe and I are getting on really well at the moment, and Erika's been nice all week. There's been no more 'Don't talk to Daisy'. Quite the opposite, in fact. Everyone's been friendly but if I speak two words to Erika, Phoebe still droops.

No, actually she doesn't now. She *hisses*.

It's a mini-explosion and quite funny.

Except that I feel bad about Erika who wants, no *needs*, a lift home with us after Drama Club. I told her I'd talk to Phoebe about it, but I haven't – yet.

Erika

Time's running out.

Thing is, I can't go to Drama Club tonight unless I can get a lift home, well to my gran's, because Mum and Dad are going to the rugby club dance. They're taking my brothers to Gran's earlier.

I suppose I need to talk to Phoebe myself – though Daisy said she would – but Phoebe's not speaking. Not to me, anyway. I've tried to be nice to her all week. I asked both of them round to my house to see my *The Wizard of Oz* DVD, and I think Daisy was going to say yes till Phoebe sort of snorted and said she has it.

I asked Daisy on Wednesday if I could have a lift home with her because my mum can only take me, but she said her mum hasn't got a car now. She always gets a lift with Phoebe both ways *and* she was having a sleepover with Phoebe this Friday.

Daisy said she'd get back to me. But here it is, Friday afternoon, and she still hasn't.

At break I asked Barney if I could have a lift with him but he said his dad's car is full already. I said I was nervous about the audition. He laughed – as if he didn't believe me – and said there'll be parts for everyone and no one will be left out. Trouble is – I couldn't say this – I don't want *any* part. Actually, I think Mum's gone off Drama Club now she's realised there will be loads of extra rehearsals to go to – on top of all my matches and practices – and she definitely won't want to take me if I'm only a Munchkin or a Winkie or a Winged Monkey.

Barney said I'd make a good Wicked Witch of the West.

I'm beginning to think he doesn't like me.

Daisy

I've been a chicken.

After school I managed to leave without talking to Erika.

But I soon wished I hadn't snuck out because right at the last minute Phoebe's dad sent a text to her mum saying he was stuck at work with the car. So she couldn't take us to Drama Club.

'Can't take us?' Phoebe *wailed*. 'But, Mum, you've got to!'

Well, I'd have wailed too if I'd been at home but, as I wasn't, I racked my brain for a solution and said, 'We'll have to ask Erika. She did offer.'

Well, Phoebe shook her head as if I'd suggested going in a car with a boa constrictor, but I told her, 'It's Erika or nothing.'

And, hoping it wasn't too late, we got

61

Phoebe's mum to ring Erika's – while we tried to keep The Smellies quiet by building brick towers for them to knock down. Actually, they were quite sweet.

Soon there was a knock on the door and Erika was on the doorstep looking ever so pleased. Her mum was outside in their car and Phoebe and I piled in the back. Erika was chatty and I did my best to chat back, even though I could feel Phoebe glowering at me.

The auditions were fun – nerve-racking but fun. At first we did some loosening-up exercises, then Lenny asked us to try different characters. He asked Phoebe to read the part of Cowardly Lion who wanted more than anything to be brave and Erika to try the part of the Tin Woodman who needs a heart. The thought *typecasting* came into my head when he asked me to try for Scarecrow.

All three of us did well, that's what I thought, and I think Lenny did too because he called us back to read a bit more. We had to do part of a scene together and by the end of it we were working well as a team – even Phoebe. Well, she was so into the part of Cowardly Lion, I think she forgot it was Erika being Tin Woodman.

It wasn't until later that things started to go wrong. The session had ended and we were outside waiting for Phoebe's dad to pick us up. I suddenly realised we were the last ones waiting and that it was ever so dark. Clouds covered the moon and the stars. The only light was a dim yellow lamp flickering above the door, and the wind was howling through the bare branches of some nearby trees. From time to time, when the wind dropped, you could hear water hitting the sides of the mill with an eerie splash, but you couldn't see the pond. You couldn't see where it began. All you

64

could see, every now and again, was a jerky shadow on the mill wall. *A tree,* I told myself, though sometimes it looked like a person.

Looking out for Phoebe's dad's car I saw a pair of red tail-lights moving down the track towards the road. Then they disappeared and there were no more after that, and no headlights coming in the opposite direction.

We were alone by a mill which some people said was haunted. Rubbish, of course, but . . .

Phoebe

We waited for ages.

I felt awful. I mean it was my dad we were waiting for. What had happened? Surely he must have left work by now?

Daisy was unusually quiet. So was Erika. In the end I said, 'I can't think where Dad's got to. Sorry.'

Erika sounded cross. 'It's freezing out here. We'd better go inside and tell Lenny.'

But Lenny had gone already. I knew he had, and when Erika tried the door – she didn't believe me, of course – she found it was locked, and Daisy said she remembered seeing him outside earlier.

'He must have thought we'd been picked up when we went to the outside loo.'

As far as we could see, which wasn't very far, there were no cars left in the car park.

My tummy started squirgling as if something bad was going to happen.

'OK.' Erika waved her mobile as if it was the answer to everything. 'There's obviously been a mix-up over times. We need to ring home – *your* home, Phoebe. What's your number?'

But when she tried to ring she couldn't get a signal and I remembered other people had said their phones didn't work here. Neither Daisy nor I had mobiles, and I started to feel panicky.

Daisy was making a big effort to keep calm, I could tell. And Erika was still being team captain.

'Right, we need a plan.' Erika looked at her watch. 'It's nine o'clock. There's obviously been a hitch. Who usually meets you guys?'

I said it was usually Mum, but Dad was going to come straight from work this evening.

'Right. That's it, isn't it?' Erika sounded super-confident. 'I bet your dad doesn't know he has to come right down the track to the mill to get us. So he's parked on the road, waiting for us. We'll just have to walk up there.'

I had to agree, though I hated being bossed around by *her*.

I said, 'We'll have to be careful we don't fall in the pond.'

There were railings round it but some of them were broken – and there was something else.

Peg Powler.

It's just a stupid legend about this girl who drowned in olden times . . . but the shadow on the mill wall kept making me think she might be around. She has these long arms and—

Enough of that! I just knew I wanted to get as far away as possible, so I set off after Erika.

Erika

'Come on, Phoebe.' I *didn't* call her Pheeble even though she looked like a frightened rabbit. 'Let's go and look for your dad.'

Anything was better than standing there doing nothing, thinking about . . . *Peg Powler* . . .

They both agreed that walking to the road was the best option, though neither of them said *Thank you, Erika. What a good idea.*

It was about half a mile, I reckoned, and would take about ten minutes. Well, it would take *me* about ten minutes. I set off at a brisk pace, hoping the other two would be able to keep up, when I tripped and hurt my foot.

Hurt isn't the word. I couldn't believe the pain. The *agony*. Or the embarrassment. I felt so stupid.

One second I was striding forward, leading

the other two. Next I was writhing on the ground with the pair of them looking down at me.

To my amazement Phoebe took charge. 'Don't move. You mustn't put any weight on the foot. It might be broken.' She'd done first aid in Brownies, she said. 'We must get help.'

Daisy was worried. 'We can't just leave her here, can we?'

'No, don't leave me!' I hated myself for crying out, but my head hurt too and, well, I didn't want to scare the others, but it was really spooky. I was sure I could see something moving by the pond.

'Erika, we're *not* going to leave you.' Daisy sounded cross, but Phoebe was more sympathetic. She was kneeling by my foot.

'Ow!' She touched it.

'Sorry, but it may just be sprained, not broken. If it is, maybe you could walk to the road if we took your weight?'

71

But when I got to my feet with their help it was still agony. There was no way I could walk that far.

'W-we'll have to go back to the mill then,' said Daisy.

She didn't sound too keen.

Nor did Phoebe. 'And h-hope for the best and that my dad comes soon. I expect he'll come looking when we don't turn up.'

I knew I should say *Just leave me here and go for help*, but I couldn't. I was sure the eerie splashing from the pond was getting louder.

The mill was about fifty metres away and we could see the yellow light glimmering. I managed to hop on my good foot with my arms round their shoulders – they nearly carried me – and when we got to the door, they lowered me carefully to the ground. Daisy got her pyjamas out of her backpack and made a cushion for my hurt foot.

Daisy said, 'Let's all look in our bags and see what else we've got.'

Soon we had a pile consisting of pyjamas; a gym shirt; gym shorts; several books, including *The Wizard of Oz*; and a squashed Mars Bar, which we shared. I insisted we shared.

Phoebe made sure we put on all the extra clothes to keep warm.

'Especially you, Erika. You must keep warm in case of shock. Put Daisy's gym kit on over your clothes.'

I must have looked like a scarecrow, but I didn't care.

Just hoped I'd scare any spooks.

Daisy

Peg Powler.

Whenever it went silent – I mean if we stopped talking – I couldn't help thinking about her. You could hear the wind howling. Or maybe a ghostly voice? Peg Powler is a legend, a drowned girl, a ghost – I may as well say it – who's supposed to hide in the pond under the slime. Sometimes, people say, she reaches out with her long white arms and grabs passers-by.

To drown them. As revenge for something.

Not true. A story. I told myself. *A ghost story. I don't believe in ghosts.*

Luckily we didn't stop talking for long, because Phoebe said the two of us must keep Erika awake in case she had concussion. Phoebe really was a heroine, a proper Florence Nightingale.

Anyway, we sat either side of Erika and talked and played games and took it in turns to read bits from *The Wizard of Oz*, which helped keep our spirits up. Luckily the light over the door stayed on – as long as we waved our arms every now and again. It was the only light because the moon stayed behind thick clouds.

Erika was brave too. I could see she was in pain but she hardly ever complained. She jumped once when a loud splashing sound came from the pond – we all did – but none of us said what we were thinking. We all kept a lookout for Phoebe's dad's car and longed to see it coming towards us. Once we thought we saw car headlights go past in the distance, on the road, but it got harder and harder to see that far. It was getting foggy. That was the trouble. It was as if the clouds were descending. Soon we could see mist *rolling* towards us, billowing like smoke but cold and wet.

I was thinking that November must be the most horrible month in the year when I saw this shape rise up and come looming out of the darkness, this human shape with arms outstretched and enormous hands . . .

Had the others seen it?

'Aaagh!' I know I cried out.

I think we all did because next thing we were clinging together, watching whatever it was coming nearer and nearer . . .

Then Erika's voice came out of the darkness saying something rude that meant, 'Go away.' I must have closed my eyes by then, and I remember thinking she was very brave – or silly to annoy the creature.

Then Phoebe started to laugh or cry in great gulping sobs. I forced myself to open my eyes and saw these huge hands gripping her shoulders . . .

Phoebe

'D-d-dad!

I recognised him first, of course, though, like the others, when I saw him coming towards us with arms outstretched I thought it was the ghost coming to get us!

It seemed ages before I noticed the sleeves of his coat. Tweed without a speck of green slime. I couldn't help screaming, 'Dad! Where have you *been*?'

Then, I have to admit, I burst into tears.

Poor Dad. He felt awful especially when we told him about Erika's injury. 'It's been one disaster after another,' he said. He'd got the time wrong – half an hour late. He'd got the pick-up place wrong, as Erika had guessed, and when he did decide that he ought to drive right down to the mill, the car wouldn't start.

'But don't worry, girls, one of my mates is on his way here in his car. I rang him. We'll go straight to the hospital. What's your parents' number, Erika?'

Daisy

It was the Best and Worst Night of My Life. I don't need to tell you why it was the worst, and you may have guessed why it was the best.

Because it changed things.

Well, you can't go through a night like that and not be changed. I think Erika and Phoebe learned to respect each other.

But it's more than that.

I didn't realise how different things were till a few weeks later when I got to school late because I'd been to the dentist. It was break, and everyone was in the playground. I scanned the yard to see who was around and spotted Erika and Phoebe, heads close together. When I got nearer I saw they were swapping Moshi cards and heard them giggling. Erika and Phoebe were giggling! Together!

And do you know what? I felt just the tiniest bit jealous and left out, till they saw me and called me over.

Actually, they've both been really friendly to me – and each other – since that night. We even play together sometimes and, when I do play with just one of them, I can't hear any hissy fits.

Oh, another thing – we all got good parts in the play. Phoebe got Cowardly Lion, Erika got

Tin Woodman and best bit last – I got Dorothy, AND they both seemed really pleased for me! We're having loads of fun rehearsing. So my plan to get my two best friends to be friendly worked after all.

Mission accomplished!

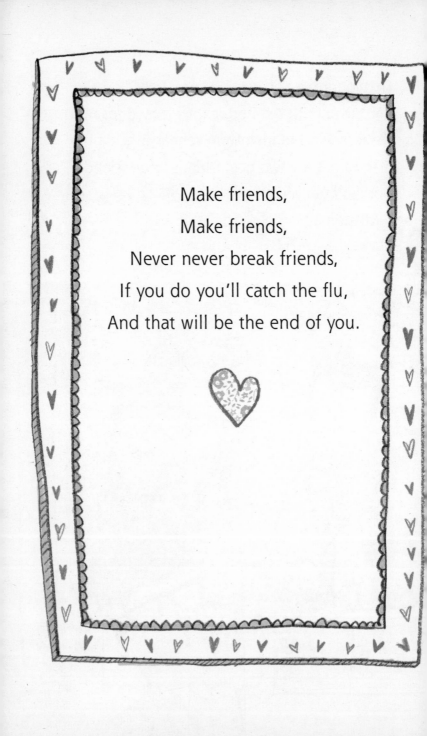

Make friends,
Make friends,
Never never break friends,
If you do you'll catch the flu,
And that will be the end of you.